g, sneezing, walking, **shouting,**
ing, **shrinking,** writing, climbing, roller-
ning, biting, drinking, **escaping,** falling,
ansforming, **wobbling,** melting, rusting,
opping, time-traveling, **dinosaur-hunting,**
ship-flying, evacuating, demonstrating,
meeting, **inventing,** whirring, rumbling,
g, creaking, slurping, beeping, squeaking,
granting, bewitching, **snake-charming,**
-breathing, egg-laying, potion-brewing,
g, hanging, racing, **crawling,** chomping,
sliding, slithering, laughing, buzzing,
nching, nibbling, **ball-chasing,** scuttling,
uddling, creeping, **exploring,** tunneling,
ng, treasure-hunting, **whizzing,** cycling,
king, **hang-gliding,** hot-air ballooning,
gliding, sinking, discovering, **dreaming.**

For everyone who loves Heffers Children's Bookshop
– P.G.

For Lily, Lucy, Emily, Jessica, Florence and Henry
– N.S.

First American Edition 2014
Kane Miller, A Division of EDC Publishing

First published in Great Britain in 2012
This edition published by permission of Random House Children's Books, London
Text © Pippa Goodhart, 2012
Illustrations @ Nick Sharratt, 2012

For information contact:
Kane Miller, A Division of EDC Publishing
PO Box 470663
Tulsa, OK 74147-0663
www.kanemiller.com
www.edcpub.com
www.usbornebooksandmore.com

Library of Congress Control Number: 2014936088

Printed and bound in China

4 5 6 7 8 9 10
ISBN: 978-1-61067-343-3

JUST IMAGINE

Words by Pippa Goodhart   Pictures by Nick Sharratt

Kane Miller
A DIVISION OF EDC PUBLISHING

Can you imagine being BIG?

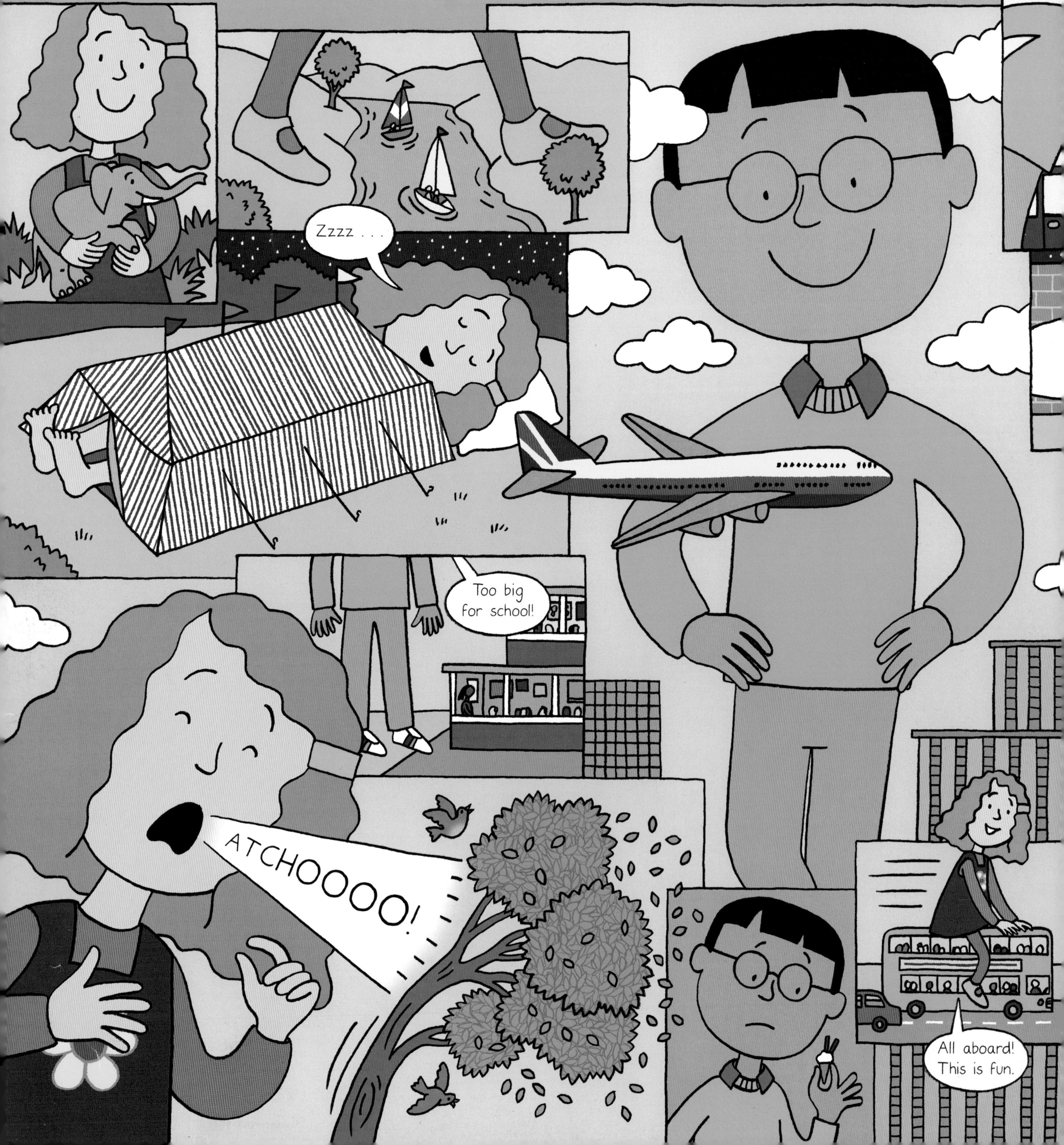

Or would you like to be small?

Imagine being made differently

– not really human at all.

Would you like

to travel through time?

Imagine being magical

– either nice or mean!

Imagine being an animal,

living in the wild.

Perhaps you'd rather be a pet, belonging to some child.

Would you like to
live underground?
Imagine how that feels.

Or would you
like to whizz around
on some kind of wheels?

or living in the sea.

Close your eyes and dream yourself

Just imagine . . . growing, **flying**, sleepi
blowing, **swimming**, eating, playing, res
skating, parent-frightening, **reading**, rur
bird-riding, washing, sailing, learning,
unraveling, **nibbling**, scaring, **stretching**,
chariot-riding, chimney-sweeping, spac
fancy-dressing, **jousting**, jiving, Viking
rolling, grinding, clanging, puffing, buzzir
huffing, **bubbling**, spell-casting, wish-
rope-climbing, magic-carpet riding, fir
Pegasus-riding, roaring, **howling**, changi
leaping, **chewing**, splashing, swinging
snorting, bounding, resting, trotting, mu
scurrying, **jumping**, walking, **feeding**,
digging, fossil-hunting, **burrowing**, pain
wheeling, **driving**, unicycling, motorbi
riding, **helicopter-flying**, diving, floating